THIS WALKER BOOK BELONGS TO:

_____

_____

_____

_____

For Alistair and Danny
A.M.

For Alexander
P.L.

First published 1987
by Walker Books Ltd
Walker House
87 Vauxhall Walk
London SE11 5HJ

This edition published 1988

Printed in Hong Kong by
Sheck Wah Tong Printing Press Ltd

British Library Cataloguing in Publication Data
Mitchell, Adrian, *1932-*
Our Mammoth.
I. Title   II. Lamont, Priscilla
823'.914[J]   PZ7
ISBN 0-7445-0931-9

OurMammoth

Written by
Adrian Mitchell

Illustrated by
Priscilla Lamont

WALKER BOOKS
LONDON

We are the Gumble Twins,
Bing and Saturday Gumble.
Bing is a gloomy boy.
Saturday is a cheerful girl.
We get along fine.

One day we took a bus to the beach.
There was nobody else on the sand.
"The wind's too wild," said Bing.
"The water looks warm," said Saturday.
So in we went.
The sea was green and cool.
The waves were tall and bumpy.

Suddenly a mountain stood up in the sea -
a blue and silver mountain.
A floating mountain of ice.
"It's an iceberg!" we shouted together.
It was our first iceberg.

The waves bumped the iceberg
    onto the beach.
"It's too slippery to climb," said Bing,
    "we'll break our backbones."
"I'll race you to the top," said Saturday.
So we climbed to the top of the
    slippy drippy iceberg and we
    looked down into the ice.

At first we wished we hadn't looked:
  we were as scared as skittles.
Deep down in the ice we saw two eyes.
Two big eyes, all brown and golden.
Two eyes, gazing up at us.
Our legs wanted to run away
  but our heads wanted to stay.
So we stayed and we stared.

The iceberg was melting
faster and faster.
Out of one end
came two curving tusks.
Then Saturday said, "Look -
an elephant's trunk."
"Can't be," said Bing.
"It's too big and too hairy."
We were too excited to
be scared any more.
We blew on the iceberg to make
the ice melt faster.

Soon all the ice had dripped
into the sand.
There stood something,
big as a lorry.

"It looks like a hill," said Bing.
"A hill with hair instead of grass,"
said Saturday.
"A hairy hill," we said together, and
we knew it was really a mammoth,
our first mammoth.

Our mammoth shivered and shook
   itself like a dog after a swim.
We jumped and squeaked.
Our mammoth stopped shaking.
It looked up at the sun.
It raised its trunk,
   then it trumpeted happily.

Our mammoth's hair was reddish-brown.
Our mammoth's hair was strong like string.
"Hello, Mammoth," we said.
It sniffed us with its trunk.

"It seems to like us," said Saturday.
"You never know," said Bing.
  We climbed up the side of our mammoth.
  We sat in the long, soft hair on its back.
  We were high up in the air.

Our mammoth made
a deep purring sound.
Then it started to walk
over the sand.
We steered our mammoth
by its ears to the field where
we live in a caravan.
We were so happy
we sang all the way -
"Here we come on our mammoth."
When cars hooted at us
our mammoth hooted back.

When the mammoth saw our mum,
    Sally Gumble, it raised its trunk and
    gave a joyful honk.
  The honk made our mum jump.
"Bing and Saturday, what on earth is that?"
"It's our mammoth," we said.
"We found it in an iceberg on the beach."

"Your mammoth is not an *it*," said Mum,
    "your mammoth is a she.
She was frozen into that
    iceberg many years ago.
She must be hungry.
What do mammoths eat?"
We didn't know
    but our mammoth knew.

The field was full of buttercups.
Our mammoth gave a snorty noise.
She picked two hundred buttercups
    with her trunk.
She popped them in her mouth.
She munched them up and
    gulped them down.

"Can we keep her?" we asked.

"Of course we can," said Mum, "she's beautiful.
What shall we call her?"

Bing said, "Sandie, because we found her
on the beach."

Saturday said, "Hilda, because she looks
like a hill."

But in the end we named her Buttercup.

Mum found a very old book in a shop.
It was called

How to Look After Your Mammoth.

It told us how to make Buttercup Pie.
The three of us ate a little of the pie
but Buttercup ate a lot.

MORE WALKER PAPERBACKS

PICTURE BOOKS
For 4 to 6-Year-Olds

Sarah Hayes
The Walker Fairy Tale Library
BOOKS ONE TO SIX
Six collections of favourite stories

Helen Craig
Susie and Alfred
THE NIGHT OF THE PAPER BAG MONSTERS
A WELCOME FOR ANNIE

PICTURE BOOKS
For 6 to 10-Year-Olds

Martin Waddell
& Joseph Wright
Little Dracula
LITTLE DRACULA'S FIRST BITE
LITTLE DRACULA'S CHRISTMAS
LITTLE DRACULA AT THE SEASIDE
LITTLE DRACULA GOES TO SCHOOL

Patrick Burston
& Alastair Graham
Which Way?
THE PLANET OF TERROR
THE JUNGLE OF PERIL

E.J. Taylor
Biscuit, Buttons and Pickles
IVY COTTAGE   GOOSE EGGS

Adrian Mitchell
& Patrick Benson
THE BARON RIDES OUT

Quentin Blake
& Michael Rosen
Scrapbooks
UNDER THE BED
HARD-BOILED LEGS
SMELLY JELLY SMELLY FISH
SPOLLYOLLYDIDDLYTIDDLYITIS

Peter Dallas-Smith
& Peter Cross
TROUBLE FOR TRUMPETS

David Lloyd
& Charlotte Voake
THE RIDICULOUS STORY OF
GAMMER GURTON'S NEEDLE

Selina Hastings
& Juan Wijngaard
SIR GAWAIN AND THE LOATHLY LADY

Martin Waddell & Dom Mansell
GREAT GRAN GORILLA
TO THE RESCUE
GREAT GRAN GORILLA
AND THE ROBBERS